THE KISS

Robin,

Enjoy fellow
mer lover! It
was so nice meeting
you!

BY: DARLENE KUNCYTES

Darlene
Kuncytes

THE MERMAID'S KISS

BY: DARLENE KUNCYTES

Copyright © at Darlene Kuncytes, 2019
All rights reserved. Printed in the United States.
Front Cover art from: Linda Boulanger, Tell Tale Book
Covers.

First Edition: June, 2019
BISAC: Fiction / Paranormal / Romance / General

10 9 8 7 6 5 4 3 2 1

All rights reserved. No part of this book may be used or reproduced, distributed, or transmitted in any form or by any means electronic or mechanical, including photocopying, recording, or by any information storage and retrieval systems, without prior written permission of the author except where permitted by law.

This is a work of fiction. The places, characters, and events portrayed in this book are products of the author's imagination or are used fictitiously. Any resemblance to actual events, locales, organizations, or real persons, living or dead, is entirely coincidental.

WORKS BY DARLENE KUNCYTES

THE SUPERNATURAL DESIRE SERIES
A Vampire's Saving Embrace: *Book One*
A Wolf's Savage Embrace: *Book Two*
Marcus' Mortal Embrace: *Book Three*

THE ANTHOLOGY NOVELLA SERIES
A Witch's Hearts Desire: *Book One*
Summer Sin: *Book Two*
Wolf Bane: *Book Three*
Magical Holiday Love: *Book Four*

STAND ALONE TITLES:
I'll Be Seeing You

Promised to a Dragon
Originally published in the **Stoking the Flames** *Anthology*

Wynter's Kiss
Originally published in the **Sinfully Delicious** *Anthology*

The Mermaid's Kiss
Originally published in the **Between the Tides** *Anthology*

ANTHOLOGY PROJECTS:

The Fountain: *Seven Extraordinary Stories by Seven of Your Favorite*

Authors

COMING SOON
Harper's Heavenly Embrace
Book Four of the Supernatural Desire Series

DEDICATION

THIS BOOK IS dedicated to my BETWEEN THE TIDES SISTERS!

This amazing group of authors are some of the most talented, giving and caring women I have ever had the pleasure to work with. Their love and support, not to mention their enormous hearts inspire and astound me each and every day. I cannot even begin to express how so very blessed I am to have you incredible souls in my heart squad!

TABLE OF CONTENTS

ACKNOWLEDGMENTS

FIRST AND FOREMOST, I want to thank you, my faithful and supportive readers. Thank you for letting me tell you my stories, and for always coming back for more! It's because of you, that I do what I do. You all are my life's blood, and you encourage and inspire me daily to keep living my dream.

I would also like to say a special thank you to some absolutely fabulous ladies who are truly my family. They may not be by blood, but they sure as hell are by love.

Andi, Marj and Linda. You wonderful spirits are always there when I need you most. NO matter what, you are a shoulder to cry on. An ear to listen to as I rant...but most importantly a friend and a sister. So, thank you girls. You know I love you to the moon and back!

THE MERMAID'S KISS

CHAPTER ONE

MARISSA HELD HER breath as she cautiously glided closer to the shoreline, being careful to keep just her head above water as she took great pains to stay hidden from the goings-on at the beach. She moved in slowly, slipping behind a large boulder near where the group of men gathered. Undetected, she allowed herself a small breath of relief as their shouts and curses reached her ears over the sound of the waves as they lapped to shore. Luckily the moon was at its fullest, and she could see the men clearly from her hiding place as they dragged an enormous hulk of a male along the beach, laughing drunkenly as they did.

The man was eerily still as he was callously tossed to the sand with no more regard than a sack of grain, and Marissa moved in a bit closer, trying her best to get a better look.

She knew she shouldn't be here. She *knew t*hat this was beyond foolish. She told herself that she should go back and leave these jackasses to their sickening games. But, for some reason, she just couldn't bring herself to do it. She stayed rooted to the spot, so to speak, holding on to the rock in a death grip as she peered from behind.

THE MERMAID'S KISS

"Arrogant, nosey bastard," she heard one of the men growl, right before lifting a heavily booted foot and kicking the body lying in the sand with such force that she swore she heard ribs crack. She winced at the impact, certain that she had detected the sound of a grunt coming from the target of the bastard's abuse. Even over the sound of the waves, she was *sure* she had heard it.

He must still be alive.

The men laughed and encouraged each other to take turns viciously beating the man as they shouted out curses like the disgusting bilge rats they were. Marissa's anger began to bubble up inside of her. No one deserved to be treated so appallingly!

She cringed as she watched one of them stomp on their victim's leg, and this time she was positive she heard his bone snap.

Marissa was all too familiar with this particular group of men. Although, referring to said cluster of degenerates as *men* was being more than generous. *Filthy beasts* would be more fitting.

They were from a rogue group of merpeople who were known to be no better than pirates. They stayed in their group and stole whatever they wanted in order to gain power. Not to mention, killed merely for the sheer pleasure of it. They got off on the rush they felt torturing and killing others. From what she had gathered, their main objective in life was to destroy other supernatural beings, thinking they would then be considered the superior species simply because of their murderous ways.

What a damn joke!

All her life she had heard the stories of these devils. Cautionary tales told to her by other merpeople of their dark, evil ways. She had been advised to take the greatest of care to stay as far from where they made their homes as she could. Never to venture too close to them.

This particular group stayed in the murky waters near the shore, and she would constantly be reminded that they were dangerous beyond anything she could ever imagine. And, even though she rarely ever ventured onto land, she knew that this group did.

Often.

It was common knowledge among her kind that these rogues enjoyed their nightly visits among the *landwalkers*. It was their opportunity to drink to excess and engage in all kinds of debauchery. Not to mention to capture and kill paranormal beings as well as humans at will, before slinking back to the sea like the scum that they were.

She couldn't tell from her vantage point exactly what type of paranormal being they were currently torturing, but by the size of the body lying there so motionless, she would have to guess either bear shifter or dragon. They tended to be the largest of the shifters, and this one was particularly huge. In fact, he was enormous. It had taken all six men to drag his prone body along the beach, and mermen were not weak by any means.

Once again, she told herself she should leave. Forget what she was seeing and get as far away from these beasts as was possible, but she still didn't move from her hiding place. Maybe it was the fact that she had never seen them at work before…or that it infuriated her to see another being suffer. She didn't know, but she found herself drifting closer to shore before her better judgement could take over. It was almost as if she was being drawn there by some unseen force. A pull that was impossible to ignore.

"What do you think we should do with him?" One of them asked.

"We kill the bastard!" Another snarled in response, who, Marissa was fairly certain, was the ring leader of this little band of dumbasses. "Dump him in the water and let the sea do her job. The sharks will eat well tonight!" He leaned down and nudged the man with his foot. "I don't think he's breathing," he informed the others matter-of-factly.

"But, wouldn't it be wise to keep him around as a bargaining chip? I'm sure his people would pay dearly for his return." One of the men standing off to the side commented.

"Are you really *that* fucking stupid?" The jack-off that had to be leader, snapped angrily. "We were lucky to have caught him off guard as it was. We sure as shit can't take the risk of keeping him alive! That would be suicidal. Although, I highly doubt that's even an option at this point, and I don't relish the thought of keeping a body around," he said, once again nudging the man with the toe of his boot. "Besides, there'll be nothing left of him by morning. His people don't need to know that he's dead."

Marissa watched as he leaned down and wrapped his finger around some type of medallion on a cord hanging from around the man's neck and yanked it off, grunting in what could only be complete satisfied arrogance, and her anger went rushing through her once again, causing her body to vibrate slightly.

"This is all we'll need," he laughed, holding his treasure up for the others to see, and the soft murmur of approval drifted on the air. "If his people doubt us, we need only to show them this. Come on, throw him to the sharks and let them take care of the trash. We have celebrating to do!"

He flicked his hand at the figure in what looked to be dismissal and headed back up the beach, leaving his cronies to lift the body and haul it to the surf.

Marissa quickly swam back a bit, careful to remain securely hidden from view as she watched the men toss the body into the waves as if dumping trash, and her anger grew. Her mood growing as dark as the waves that crashed so violently to shore. No creature deserved to be treated that abominably!

She dropped beneath the surface and swam towards where they had dumped him, knowing full well that the rip-tides in this area were particularly vicious and she was pretty damned sure that was most-likely one of the main reasons the group of mermen had chosen it. The body would be swept out to sea in a matter of seconds if she didn't hurry.

She spotted him sinking toward the bottom, his body moving jerkily as the tides pulled and tossed their treat. She moved in to take a closer look, stunned at just how large he actually was. He was a solid wall of muscle, with strong, powerful features, and she couldn't help but think what a waste of a fine specimen it was. The man was incredibly handsome.

Marissa jerked back in shock when she saw, what she was fairly sure was, the man opening his eyes for just the briefest of moments, but she couldn't be certain if it was simply a trick of the moonlight bouncing off of the water or not.

She moved in closer, this time within inches of his flawless, perfect face and narrowed her eyes. Nothing. His lids were tightly shut, framed by thick, black lashes.

It must have been her imagination. Lord knew the light filtering through the waters could be deceiving.

She hovered near as she studied him intently, trying to decide what to do. It felt so wrong to just leave him to the mercy of the ocean depths. Not to mention what the sharks would do, she thought with a shudder.

Should she do something with the body?

Or, should she be smart and stay out of it?

The thought of him being torn apart and blindly devoured in a feeding frenzy made her stomach tighten into knots. No one deserved that.

But, what could she really do? She had no idea of his identity or even where he was from. Or who and *what,* for that matter, he and his people were.

Just where was she supposed to take his body?

She realized there was nothing she could do for him, and was just about to turn and swim away, when she saw bubbles slipping from between his full, perfect lips and she *swore* on Neptune's triton that she saw his mouth move.

A single movement. A word. A plea.

Help.

Not giving herself a moment to think about what a possibly, monumentally, *dumb-assed* risk she was taking, she grabbed hold of his forearm and took off. Swimming for all she was worth towards the only place she could think of taking him where they would be safe. A secret cave she frequented. It wasn't much, but there was air to be had, and more importantly…it was well hidden.

As far as Marissa knew, she was the only one who had ever been to this particular cavern. In all the years that she had been taking refuge there since she had stumbled upon it, she had never seen any indication at all of anyone else ever having been inside; so, she knew that it was the best place to take him. She would be able to check to make sure that what she *believed* she was seeing was real, and hopefully help him if it was. Give him a safe place to heal.

Unlike most merpeople, Marissa didn't inherently despise all other paranormal beings. In fact, she had always been fascinated by them and their ways. Although, not curious enough to venture onto land that often as others of her kind did, but she wasn't going to miss the opportunity to help one in distress. Especially not one as fascinating as this particular creature. She just couldn't seem to stop herself from getting involved.

But, hadn't that always been her biggest fault?

THE FIGURE WATCHED as the mermaid deftly pulled the body through the water, completely oblivious to the eyes that followed her. She was much too enraptured with her catch. Deciding that his leader would be very interested to know where she was taking him, he followed at a distance, his excitement growing with the thought of how valuable this information would be to his fellow mermen, and what riches he might possibly collect with this little tidbit.

If nothing else, it would score him some brownie points.

MARISSA BROKE THE surface of the water in the middle of the cave, swimming to the edge in the darkness from memory, waiting for her eyes to adjust. Using all of her strength, she pushed the massive figure in front of her and slid him up onto the cavern floor, her arms shaking from the effort. Even with the buoyancy of the water to help ease the load, the dead weight of solid muscle was *heavy.*

She moved away from where he lay and dipped below the surface once again before slipping up next to him. She closed her eyes and waited for her legs to appear, loving the freedom the appendages always seemed to give her.

She adored her ocean home. She truly did. But, if she were to be completely honest with herself, there *were* advantages to having legs. Besides, she thought as a small smile flitted across her lips, they weren't half bad to look at, really. Long and shapely, they were quite fetching. Not to mention, that aside from being pretty, she really did like the feel of them and the freedom they seemed to give. It was one of the reasons she frequented her hiding place. She could enjoy her legs here undisturbed, and not have to go anywhere near the *landwalkers.*

If the land above, and the creatures who inhabited it, didn't scare her so much, she *might* have spent more time up there among them. Instead, she made this her sanctuary.

Her smiled faded as the memory of the last time she had dared to venture onto the land flashed before her, and she quickly shoved it away, concentrating instead on the still form sprawled out beside her, as she fought the temptation to run her fingers over his strong, chiseled face.

She stood and moved around behind him, slipping her hands beneath his arms and pulling him further into the cavern and away from the water. Not an easy task whatsoever.

She leaned him against a nearby boulder, worn smooth from years of erosion, and knelt down. He was deathly still, and from what she could see, his skin held an almost ashen color to it.

Not a good sign.

She pressed her ear against his chest and she listened intently, trying to detect the faint sound of a heartbeat above the noise of the lapping of the water.

But there was nothing.

She hesitated a moment, fighting an inner battle with herself that was making her heart do a little flip against her ribs.

Should she?

Marissa only hesitated only a second more before pressing her lips against his and blowing a life-saving breath into his lungs. She didn't want to give herself a moment to chicken out.

One of the powers that the merpeople possessed, was the ability to breathe life back into a drowning or lost soul, but it was a gift that was to be used in very rare instances, and was fundamentally frowned upon by her people.

Believing that death came when it was supposed to, it was stressed that they should never interfere in the lives or deaths of others. Especially that of the *landwalkers*. They believed their power should only be used on their own kind, and only *then* when it was absolutely necessary. To the merpeople, the destinies of humans and other paranormal beings were not of their concern.

She knew she was going against all of their beliefs, and if found out, it could cause immense trouble for her, but Marissa had always had a soft spot for creatures in need. And she wasn't going to change now. She couldn't care less if her people believed that this ability would be wasted on saving the life of another paranormal being. He needed help.

He needed *her.*

Marissa jerked back when he spasmed violently and started to choke, coughing up the water in his lungs. He rolled to his side and expelled what seemed to be half the ocean, and she quickly stood and ran toward the back of the cave where she kept some clothing stashed away for the times she dared to come to her quiet place. Or if she planned on venturing on land. It had been forever it seemed, since she had done that, but she still liked to use her legs and dress up every now and again, loving the feel of the different fabrics against her skin.

Sometimes it was nice pretending to be someone else, and over the years she had stashed away quite a few human treasures.

Marissa could hear him hacking and coughing as she hastily donned a sundress and grabbed the lantern and waterproof matches in one of the bags she kept stashed away here.

She dashed back to where he lay and lit the lantern, illuminating the space in a flickering, golden glow that only served to enhance his incredibly handsome features.

He was so strikingly beautiful that it took her breath away, and even though she knew that she shouldn't be thinking it, she couldn't seem to help herself. It was just a fact that couldn't be ignored.

He turned and caught her eyes and she was thrown by the intensity of their silver depths. She had never seen eyes that color before. They were startling, like mercury.

She could see a muscle in his perfectly square jaw twitching dangerously as he seemed to size her up, struggling to get to his feet, but the broken bones were effectively preventing that from happening.

"Don't try to stand," she instructed quickly, her hand unconsciously reaching out and touching his shoulder, and damned if it didn't feel as if she had laid her fingers upon solid granite. "You're badly hurt."

He pulled back from her touch, glaring at her as if she were a disgusting piece of filth. "Just who in the *Hell* are you?" He growled, and she knew beyond a doubt that the husky timber of his voice was not due to all the water he had just coughed up. That was natural.

He looked ready to pounce, and she was pretty sure if he did, she'd be done for, even with his many injuries. He had at least a foot on her and most likely well over a hundred pounds.

Not to mention that he looked ready to kill.

She scuttled back slightly, lifting her arms in an attempt to show that she meant him no harm. She could see the cuts and bruises marring his face and body, and her heart did another little flip inside her ribs. This time with empathy. She would never understand how beings could be so horrendously cruel to one another.

"Please," she whispered, her voice seeming to stick in her throat. She attempted to clear it and took a breath. "I promise, I won't hurt you."

He chuffed sarcastically, as if the mere idea of her causing him any harm was funny as hell, before his eyes broke free of hers and began skimming across her features and down her body in a slow, thorough appraisal, bringing a rush of heat to wherever they happened to venture and she felt herself frown, her temper beginning to flare up with his blatant perusal of her.

He sure as hell had some damn nerve ogling her like a well-fed tuna when she had saved his sorry ass from certain death!

CHASE BASTAINE CLENCHED his jaw, trying his best to contain his fury as he watched the woman in front of him cautiously, ignoring the shooting stab of pain from his battered body, even though it was screaming at him to take notice. Those sons of bitches had sure as hell done a number on him, and he was thoroughly pissed off and wanted blood!

Damn filthy bottom feeders!

When he made another move to rise, his ribs screamed out in agony like he had never experienced before, making him dizzy and bile to rise in his gut, not to mention the blaze of pure fire that shot through his leg; but he sure as hell wasn't about to let this little slip of a woman know that.

Not until he knew exactly who in the hell she was, and just what her part in all of this bullshit was.

She made a move back towards him and once again reached out a delicate hand, but he snarled in return, causing her to pull it back, almost as if she had been burned.

"Who in the fuck *are* you," he repeated venomously, although the power behind his words was sorely lacking as the overwhelming feeling that he was about to lose consciousness hit him like a sledge hammer between the eyes, but he fought it for all he was worth.

Until he knew just what in the hell had happened, and who this woman was, and *where* his damned attackers were, he needed to stay focused. He couldn't let himself succumb to the darkness trying to overtake him. No matter how much he wanted to fall into its sweet embrace.

"Please. I…I only want to help you," he heard her murmur, her voice soft and eerily soothing, almost *musical,* and he found himself relaxing the tiniest bit. Either that, or his exhaustion was winning. "The men who…who hurt you, are gone. They believe you were dead."

He studied her silently a moment, trying to clear his aching head enough to try and read if she was being truthful or not, but it was proving to be damned hard, if not impossible. He felt as if he had been run over by a truck.

A very *large* truck.

"Why?" He asked finally, and noticed that she seemed to swallow with what looked to be difficulty.

"Why, *what?*" she questioned, and Chase fought off a rousing round of nausea as he struggled to keep his eyes focused on the delicate little beauty.

Christ, he wasn't even sure how much longer he was going to be able to hold on.

The rushing of blood to his ears was deafening. Not to mention the pressure behind his eyes that it was causing.

"Listen, *Sweetheart*," he croaked out icily, "I don't know just who in the hell you are, but I need answers, and you *know* what I mean. I feel like shit, and I'm not in the mood to play games." He slowly moved his head and glanced around the dank cavern a moment as he pushed away the feeling of claustrophobia that was descending on him before glaring at her once again. "Where are we?"

"It's…it's a cave. It's safe," she stammered in response.

"How did I get here?"

"I brought you here when they threw you into the water."

"Do you know who *they* are?" He threw back at her, more than just a bit irritably.

This back and forth was beginning to sap what little strength he had left, and he closed his eyes a moment to try and gather some momentum before opening them just in time to see her nodding slowly.

"Who?" He snarled, a part of him wanting to lash out at her. To grab her and just shake that pretty little body of hers until she told him everything.

He *knew* that she had to be a part of this! Why else would she have brought him here? She had most likely been given the task of watching over him until those bastards returned from wherever they had gone.

Although, he silently thought, as he once again looked her up and down, even in his battered state, this beautiful little nymph didn't stand a chance against him if he chose to attack. He would be able to snap her like a twig.

He glared at her.

Waiting.

His patience was being pressed beyond its limits and he bit back the growl that hovered at his lips. He was done playing twenty questions. He wanted answers.

It wasn't even that he was angry with her exactly. He was just thoroughly frigging pissed off that he had let his guard down long enough to have been attacked in the first place. He had been fucking *blindsided* and he didn't like it!

At all.

And if she was a part of the group who had jumped him…

His hand instinctively went to his chest, looking for his amulet, only to discover it gone and he exploded once again.

"Where is it?" he hissed between teeth that were so tightly clenched that a small part of him wondered why they hadn't shattered like glass. This time he did reach out and grabbed her by the wrist, pulling her down to her knees beside him as a frightened squeak erupted from her.

"What?" She breathed out as she attempted to pull her arm from his grip, but it was futile, and she knew it. He could see the panic building in her eyes. "Where's *what?*"

"The stone of *Dragaan.*" He snapped back as tiny stars began to dance and spin crazily in front of him, which he was certain were caused from the energy his rage was sucking from him. He dropped her wrist to press his palms against his eyes in an attempt to stop their spinning.

When he finally looked back up at her, it was in time to see her eyes deepen from that lovely aqua to an almost emerald green with what could only be taken for her own anger, and she scuttled back out of his reach, her chest heaving with indignation as she plopped down on her ass and rubbed her wrist.

"Do you mean your necklace?" She asked, her eyes narrowing as her full, pouty little mouth set itself into a tight frown.

"Yes!" He all but roared, and the stars happily swimming in front of him suddenly burst into blinding flashes of brightly colored light, and he felt the cave beginning to spin and lurch around him, causing a wave of nausea to hit him.

The last thing he remembered before everything went black was her musical voice telling him that the men who had jumped him had taken it with them.

MARISSA WATCHED IN stunned silence as his eyes rolled back in his head and he collapsed to the cavern floor, his huge hulk of a body so incredibly still that she feared he was dead, this time for real. She moved in a bit closer, crawling over to where he lay only to breathe a sigh a relief when she heard the faint sound of air whistling through his lungs.

She stood and moved to where she kept her stuff stashed away, and grabbed a few blankets. She bunched one up to place under his head, the other she draped over his body, noticing how it barely covered his shins, and figured he had to be well over six foot.

She paced the cave, wondering what she should do next. The man was an insufferable arrogant ass, and seemed to be able to push her buttons with just a single word.

But...he was also a creature in need of help, and she couldn't forget that. He needed to rest and to have his wounds tended to. She didn't have any medical supplies down here to speak of, and glanced down toward the dark space at the back of the cavern, wondering if she dared to venture on land.

Just the thought of going above caused a pit to begin to form in her stomach, and she held her breath, trying to work up the courage to do what she knew had to be done. She couldn't take the risk of his wounds getting infected, and he would need something to eat, and fresh water...

She anxiously nibbled at her bottom lip as she debated on whether or not she could do it. Could she really go above among the *landwalkers* again? It had been years since she had, and she knew that it could only have gotten worse up there; but she would not let her fear keep her from helping someone in need. No matter how abominably they had behaved.

Marissa had been smart enough over the years to have had the forethought to sell some of the gold coins found on the ocean floor for human money. Keeping it safely stashed away for her journeys to land, she would purchase the things that would catch her eye. She wasn't sure how much was left, she hadn't bother to count it in a very long time, but she was sure there was more than enough.

She stared down at him, her body beginning to grow clammy from nerves, and willed herself to relax. He would be out for a while, she was sure, and if she only grabbed the bare necessities, she could be back before he woke.

"Son of a sea-witch," she grumbled as she stomped over to where she kept a pair of shoes and a jacket and slipped them on. "Just the bare minimum," she whispered to herself as she took off down the passage that led to the land above. "In and out. It'll be easy. Nothing to worry about at all. You can do this." She rambled on to no one in particular.

Marissa knew that even if he did wake in her absence, he wouldn't be able to walk, let alone find the small crevice that led to the beach above, and he sure as heck was in no condition to swim it. Besides, she'd be back long before that, even though the growing dampness of her palms begged to differ. She straightened her back and pushed on, refusing to let the butterflies roiling around in her belly stop her.

CHAPTER TWO

MARISSA COULD HEAR the sounds of laughter, curse words and music drifting on the air as she made her way closer to the small beach town. At this time of night, the bars would most likely be filled to capacity. The *landwalkers* would be dancing and drinking to excess, looking for the easiest warm body to take home for the night.

Some things never changed.

She forced herself to tune out the sound as she forged ahead, the smell of shrimp boiling hit her nose and caused her tummy grumble with neglect. She realized that she had not eaten anything at all that day, and was famished.

She shoved her hunger aside and headed towards the small general store she remembered at the edge of the town square, hoping they would have everything she needed. She didn't relish the thought of having to go looking for another. The very last thing she wanted to do was wander about among the *landwalkers*. Especially in the dark.

It will only be a few moments. In and out. Just get what you need, and you can go back.

In and out.

THE MERMAID'S KISS

She silently repeated the words to herself over and over again as she walked along, hoping to ease the unease that was building up inside her with each step that she took, as if by saying them, they would keep her protected, safe from the dangers that lurked about in the shadows in places like this.

The ding of a bell announced her arrival as she stepped through the entrance of the store, which seemed much larger than she remembered.

The lone cashier looked up from the magazine she was perusing with disinterest for the briefest of moments before glancing back down and flipping the page with an audible snap.

She was a young, pretty girl, and if Marissa had to guess, she would say no more than eighteen years old. Much too young to be working alone at this time of night. She pushed the thought from her mind and headed down the first aide aisle, hastily grabbing whatever she could find. Bandages, alcohol, all the while repeating her mantra.

In and out. In and out.

By the time she had gotten everything she needed, including some water and food, she was more than ready to head back. The paranoia creeping up on her was getting worse, and she was finding it harder and harder to breathe.

Like a fish out of water.

She would have laughed at the thought if she wasn't so uncomfortable, and quickly paid for her purchase before dashing from the store and back down to the beach, knowing full well that if anyone had seen her or paid attention to her, they would have thought her stark raving mad for running away as she had. Either that, or that she was possibly a thief, running from the scene of the crime. Thankfully, the people of the small town were much too busy throwing back shots and having a good time to worry about her.

MARISSA SILENTLY SLIPPED THROUGH the opening in the rocks, and pulled her bags in behind her, hurrying back to where she had left her guest, and praying that he hadn't woken.

As she had hoped, he was still out cold, and she quickly set to work cleaning and dressing his wounds as best she could, all the while making a sound of disapproval deep in her throat, furious at the damage those animals had done to him.

The best she could tell, he had several broken ribs, and his leg had been badly damaged, and she realized that she *had* heard it snap. She cringed at the sight of the bone protruding from his shin, and shoved away the urge to burst into tears with an audible swallow as she did what she could to set it. It wounded her to think that someone would be so cruel as to inflict such brutality on another being, and the realization that it had been her own people who had chosen to inflict such damage, cut her to the quick.

She wrapped pieces of cloth around the makeshift splint with slow and deliberate care, doing her best not to jostle him more than was necessary.

Finally, she leaned back a bit, wiping the sweat from her brow and studying her handiwork. It seemed fairly straight, and she was more than just a little grateful that he had stayed unconscious during the whole process. The thought of the pain he would have experienced as she set his leg frightened the pearls out of her.

Not to mention the fury his discomfort would most surely have caused, and *that* scared her more than anything. No matter *how* handsome the man was, he was still intimidating as hell, and until he realized that she was only trying to help him, she wanted him to remain as anger free as possible.

Marissa set her medical supplies off to the side and began building a small fire. Luckily there was plenty of oxygen in the cavern and the way it was set up would keep anyone with prying eyes from seeing the smoke. Still, she kept the fire small, just enough to warm the area up a bit to help him dry out, and cook up some food when he woke.

When she had the fire burning steadily, she sat back down opposite of where he lay, and pulled her knees up to her chest, resting her chin on them. She sat there quietly, studying the man lying there so still, only the movement of his chest indicating that he was alive.

He was fascinating.

She still couldn't be one-hundred percent sure exactly *what* type of paranormal being he was, but she knew that he was definitely *not* human. And, he had asked where the stone of *Dragaan* was, so if she had to make an educated guess, she was leaning heavily toward dragon shifter, which only piqued her interest all the more.

She had never met an actual dragon shifter in the flesh, but their legend was infamous far and wide. They were considered to be the highest tier of the paranormal realm. Warriors, leaders and protectors by nature, they were also known to be fiercely loyal to their people. Their quick tempers and sheer brute strength were something that was also to be feared by others in their realms, and it was said they just couldn't seem to be tamed.

She had heard the tales over the years. Tales of their strong wills, and how they ruled their clans with a strength and intelligence that was admired and revered.

Would that group of asshats been stupid enough to have messed with a dragon? She silently wondered, and instantly realized they would have.

Marissa pulled her dry hair over her shoulder and unconsciously began toying with the strands before pulling it into a nice fat braid. A habit she had picked up as a child whenever she was distracted. She jumped in surprise when he moaned, shifting his massive frame to the side facing her, and she held her breath.

It seemed her guest was waking. She only hoped he was in a somewhat better mood.

CHASE OPENED ONE eye and looked at the beautiful little sprite staring back at him so intently. Her incredible eyes wide. Good Gods, but she was lovely, and the thought that she could be one of *them* hit him hard for some reason. He glanced down and realized that she…or *someone* had bandaged him up and wondered just what in the flying fuck her deal was.

"Where is my necklace," he ground out, although his voice held no conviction in it whatsoever. He knew it was weak and no more than a pitiful hoarse whisper, and he realized that he was parched. It freaking felt as if he had been chewing on sandpaper.

He watched as she reached over beside her and pulled a bottle of water from the bag sitting there and almost allowed himself a moan of gratitude.

Almost.

She moved a bit closer to where he lay and held the bottle out to him, much like you would hold out a piece of meat to a stray dog, not knowing if it was rabid or not.

Chase took her offering and tried to move into a sitting position, but his ribs screamed in protest. Ignoring them, he clenched his jaw and struggled through the pain, acutely aware of her eyes on him every pain filled second.

When he had stationed himself into something somewhat resembling an upright position, he twisted off the cap and downed the water, thinking that nothing had ever tasted so blasted good.

"Easy," he heard her instruct him softly. Not a demand, simply a warning to be careful.

He finished the bottle and set it aside, glancing down at his leg before looking back up at her, catching her gaze. "Did you do that?" He asked, motioning to the make-shift splint.

"Yes."

"Why?"

He couldn't help but notice that her entire body stiffened as her full lips turned down into a frown. "What do you mean…*why?"* She huffed; the exasperation clear in her voice. "I wasn't about to let you suffer and die."

"I figured that your *friends* wanted me dead."

He was finding it extremely difficult to talk, his ribs were screaming out in protest with every word, but he wasn't about to let up. He wanted answers.

She stood and began to move about the cave, her movements quick and jerky, albeit still as graceful as sin, like

23

those of a dancer, and he knew that he had hit a nerve. She was irritated as hell, yet still exquisitely beautiful. Her thick, golden hair hung down in a glossy braid, and her heart-shaped face, which held those striking aqua eyes, was pure perfection.

Christ. Her eyes were the color of the sea on a vibrant morning.

Chase watched as she grabbed another bag and began taking out what looked to be food items.

"I thought I made it perfectly clear to you," she pushed out, more than just a bit irritably as she sat back down beside the fire. "They are *not* my friends."

"Well, then, would you mind telling me just who in the hell *you* are then? And, whether or not you have any knowledge whatsoever of those bastards who jumped, or where they went. Jesus, I'd even settle for what *direction* they headed at this point. Give me something."

"My name's Marissa," she informed him, and he couldn't help but think that the name fit her to perfection. Soft and smooth, it was musical and rolled off the tongue like warm honey. "And I know *of* the men who attacked you. I just don't know them *personally.*"

Feeling that he was at least getting somewhere, he pushed himself up a little further, resting against the large boulder at his back. "Who are they?" He asked, a little more harshly than he had intended, but by God, he wanted *blood.* "I sensed they were mermen," he offered, his disgust rising like bile. "Filthy bottom feeders."

MARISSA DID HER very best to hide the gasp of surprise that sprang to her lips at his obvious ignorance and hatred of her kind, biting back the angry retort that she so wanted to unleash on his arrogant ass.

Good grief! Just where in the hell did Mr. High and Mighty get off with his puffed-up, superior attitude! If it wasn't for this filthy "bottom feeder," he'd be rotting at the bottom of the sea, being picked at by the crabs!

She knew in that moment, and without a doubt in her mind, that he was indeed a dragon shifter. Bear shifters weren't usually *that* entitled.

Or blatantly egocentric.

"Did you also happen to *sense* that *I'm* also a bottom feeder," she snarled at him, her face flushing with heat as her temper simmered. "You have really got some damn nerve."

"I didn't mean *you* specifically," he offered half-heartedly. "But, if I am to be brutally honest, I really didn't think much of merpeople as a whole before tonight. Perhaps I am judging a bit prematurely since I also haven't dealt with many of you before now either, but you have to agree that my introduction to your kind has been nothing to write home about."

"Well, gee whiz," she hissed, unable to hide her contempt. "That's so awfully magnanimous of you. Damn puffed-up dragon." She finished under her breath, and swore she saw a small smile lift the corners of his battered mouth.

Ass-hat.

Marissa swallowed back her fury and hastily slapped together a sandwich for him, shoving it in his direction with another bottle of water before making one for herself. It wasn't fancy, but it was *something*.

Not that the overinflated jerk deserved it.

CHASE TOOK HER offering with a silent nod, forcing himself to take a bite. He wasn't the least bit hungry, but he knew enough to know that if he wanted to heal, he needed to eat and build up his strength. Not to mention, he didn't want to offend his hostess. Although, he seemed to have done a pretty fine job of that already. He sure as hell wasn't about to add fuel to the already burning fires until he got the answers he sought. He wasn't an imbecile.

"Thank you," he mumbled between bites before cracking open, and downing, his second bottle of water. For some reason, he was still parched. "I apologize if I came across as rude," he offered, this time with a bit more sincerity.

Her eyes met his and held with a subtle confidence that he couldn't help but admire, and that full, pouty mouth of hers softened just the tiniest bit as she seemed to study him, almost as if she were sizing him up.

"Apology accepted," she replied finally, although he couldn't help but notice that her words were still a bit clipped and somewhat flat.

He wasn't about to try and fool himself into believing that she was being completely honest. He knew that he had offended her.

Her eyes narrowed, and she leaned forward. "So, was I right?" She asked.

"About?"

"Dragon shifter?"

He swallowed the last bite of his sandwich and grinned in spite of himself, not wanting to admit that it *had* done his body a world of good to eat something. He was feeling stronger by the minute.

"Right on the nose," he chuckled, and saw what could only be described as excited curiosity flare up in her eyes.

"Wicked," she breathed, so quietly that he barely heard her, and this time he couldn't help himself, he choked out a laugh, then instantly winced at the pain it caused. "You should really rest," she said, standing and heading toward the back of the cavern, and he found himself wondering how far back it went.

This sure as hell wasn't anything near a five-star resort, and a part of him was curious as to why she chose to bring him here. Was it merely convenience? Or was there some other, darker reason?

What exactly, was the story behind this fascinating little mermaid's need to hide out? He watched as she flitted about the cavern, so graceful that it was almost magical, and he discovered himself thinking that he wanted to know more about her.

He was about to question her, when he realized that his exhaustion was getting the better of him and he felt himself drifting off. His body begging for relief.

MARISSA WATCHED AS the dragon shifter's body relaxed with the sleep Overtaking him. Taking the opportunity to try and get a bit of rest herself, she grabbed another blanket and eased herself down against one of the walls, far enough away that she felt safe enough to close her eyes, yet close enough to hear him if he moved.

It seemed as if he was warming up to her a bit. The fact that he was taking food from her was a huge step, but she knew that he was still wary of her, and a part of her understood why.

She couldn't say that she blamed him. Not really. She couldn't say for certain how trusting she would be if the situation were reversed.

Marissa pulled the blanket up to her chin and sighed, closing her eyes, she began to drift off to sleep, wondering how she was going to prove to the dragon shifter that not all of her people were scum. She knew that it wasn't going to be easy, and really had no idea *why* it even mattered, but to her, it did. She didn't want him hating her kind solely because of a few rotten oysters.

CHAPTER THREE

CHASE OPENED HIS eyes slowly, giving himself time to adjust, and immediately sought out the beautiful little water sprite. He found her leaning against the wall opposite of where he sat, fast asleep.

Even in the semi-darkness of the cave, he could see the beauty of her features, and he was thankful that dragon shifters had such good vision. He was thoroughly enjoying the view.

He was feeling stronger by the moment, and allowing himself to sleep had definitely helped. His leg was still throbbing like a bitch, but from what he could tell, it had been broken clean through and that was going to take a bit longer. At least his ribs weren't screaming out in agony with each breath he took now.

Progress.

He needed to heal as quickly as possible and find those good for nothing bastards. Hopefully, with enough time, she would be willing to give him the help that he sought. It would be nice to have inside assistance.

He just had to remember to tread lightly. He knew that he could be quick-tempered and snappy, but it was the dragon way, and it was going to take him time to learn to rein it in.

If there was one thing that was one hundred percent for sure, it was that Chase Bastaine was a formidable leader, and did not like letting someone else take that position, and it usually caused him to come across as cold. He promised himself that he would go easy with this one.

Chase watched in fascination as the creature in question made a sound in her sleep that was almost a sigh before she shifted, her eyes fluttering as she woke.

And it was enchanting.

No matter how many times he told himself to look away, he just couldn't seem to tear his eyes from the captivating sight playing out before him as she stretched her arms above her head, the blanket she had wrapped so carefully around her falling to her waist as her chest heaved out to the point of distraction. It wasn't done intentionally, but it was a wonder to watch. It was honest and easy, and he shivered.

He may be battered and bruised, but he was damn well still a man!

MARISSA NOTICED INSTANTLY the way he was watching her as she stretched, and grew flushed. She reasoned that it was due solely because of the intensity of his gaze. Who wouldn't feel completely exposed with someone *staring* at them like that!

"How are you feeling?" she croaked out, trying to ignore the feeling of self-consciousness that was washing over her and spreading through her entire body. She only truly felt comfortable in the water, and his eyes on her so intently was disconcerting. It was throwing her off her game. Not that she really had any game to speak of.

She stood and moved over to her bag, desperate to appear unfazed. She took out two bottles of water and handed him one which he accepted with a grateful nod. His eyes caught hers, and it was as if all the oxygen was suddenly sucked out of the cave and she fought to catch the breath that had hitched in her throat.

She busied herself with trying to stoke the nearly non-existent fire back to life before trying to throw together something that loosely resembled breakfast.

All the while she was painfully aware of his gaze following her every move.

"I seem to find myself in need of your assistance," she heard him say and stopped cold. She turned from her task and looked over at him with surprise.

She *knew* that this couldn't be an easy request for him to make. It was more than obvious that he was a strong and powerful man who did not take kindly to having to rely on the help of strangers.

Especially not from a lowly bottom feeder.

Marissa bit back her snarky reply and watched him a moment in silence. His discomfort was more than obvious, and she couldn't help but take a small amount of pleasure from watching him squirm. He thought he was superior, and perhaps in some ways he was, but the man needed a lesson in humility and treating others with respect.

Just because he had a run-in and had been jumped by some of the worst examples of her kind, didn't mean they were all horrible creatures. It was like with any beings that

31

wandered the earth, there was good and there was bad, and she hated that he just assumed that they were *all* thieves and scum.

Ass!

When she figured that he had sweated long enough, she handed him his food and sat down opposite of where he sat, the small fire suddenly flaring up between them as if she had poured gasoline on it, and she found it strangely fitting somehow.

"And, just what is it that you need…" she trailed off, eyeing him a moment. He hadn't even bothered to tell her his name, and here he was asking for her help. "Do you have a name, by the way?" she asked. "Or do I simply call you *dragon-shifter*?"

"Chase," he offered with a half grin that nearly stopped her heart. It was smooth, and sexy, and it made him appear incredibly roguish. "Chase Bastaine, but please, call me Chase."

"Okay, Chase. What exactly do you need from me?"

"I need you to tell me where I can find the men who attacked me," he responded bluntly.

She could see the hatred ignite in his eyes, and she knew beyond any shadow of doubt that he was planning to kill them.

"You do realize that you are in no condition to go *anywhere* at the moment?" she responded, glancing down at his leg for good measure. It was obvious that he was on the mend, but he wasn't anywhere near well enough to go traipsing about seeking revenge.

"As I'm painfully aware," he countered softly, but there was no mocking in his words. "But as a dragon, I will heal fairly quickly. I don't know if," he stumbled, a hint of red coming to his cheeks as he self-edited, "if *your* kind is the same as mine."

Marissa knew that he'd been about to say *bottom feeders.* He'd caught himself in time, and a part of her almost appreciated the gesture. He seemed to be genuinely trying not to offend her. But, he was also asking her to lead him to massacre a group of her people, and she wasn't sure how she felt about it exactly.

Yes, they were disgusting, useless, bilge rats who cared nothing about common decency and were an ugly festering boil on the bottoms of all merpeople...but they were *still* her people.

Could she really just lead them to slaughter? No matter how much better their world would be if they were wiped from it?

"I'll need some time to think about it," she responded, feeling a pit growing deep in her gut.

He nodded stiffly, and she knew that he wasn't used to being denied any request, but she would not betray her people rashly. She watched as he shifted a bit to sit up straighter and noticed tiny beads of perspiration form across his forehead from the effort that it was taking.

Marissa grabbed another bottle of water and the aspirin she had purchased.

"I'm fine," he husked irritably, waving away her offering, his mouth set in a tight line of pain, and she huffed right back at him.

Stubborn fool.

"Don't you need to go sink ships or something?" He hissed between clenched teeth, and she just wanted to spit.

"As a matter of fact, I *don't,*" she snapped back, his mood swings beginning to grate on her nerves. "I've already reached my limit for the week!"

She knew in part his anger was because he was in pain, and most likely feeling helpless, and she *had* taken a bit of a holier than though attitude with *needing to think about helping him,* when she knew damned well that she was going to.

Those men needed to be stopped.

By whatever means possible, and she knew it deep down in the recesses of her soul. They were despicable animals who put no value on life. They only valued power.

It still didn't give him the right to speak to her that way.

"Why are you such an insufferable ass?" She asked, her eyes locking onto his with defiance as she glared.

CHASE WAS SILENT for a very long moment, his stare returning hers without hesitation, and he realized that he was taking his anger and frustration out on her, and it wasn't fair. She deserved better. She had been nothing but kind to him, and he was behaving like a boorish entitled piece of shit.

"I *am* being an ass," he conceded with a sigh. "Once again, I apologize. I'm just…"

"An arrogant, pretentious jerk?" She jumped in, but he would have been hard pressed not to notice the small grin that was beginning to form at the corners of her mouth, and he had to give her props. She certainly took no prisoners.

"If you insist," he countered, returning her grin, and it was as if the air around them had suddenly lightened. "I don't like being out of commission. It darkens my usually winning personality."

"Pfft. Winning personality, my tail! Have you actually *met* you?" She threw back at him, and he couldn't hold back his laughter any longer.

It erupted from him and filled the cavern. Echoing off the walls.

She certainly was a feisty little thing, and no matter how horrendous he felt, he found himself enjoying sparing with her. She was not only beautiful, but she was witty and playful, and his opinion of her species was definitely on the up-swing.

"I have," he chuckled good-naturedly. "And I'm really not that bad once you get to know me."

She made the cutest little sound of disbelief as she rolled her lovely aqua eyes and offered him the water and bottle of aspirin again.

This time he took it.

His leg was throbbing, and he knew it was because his bone was beginning to fuse, and although one of the benefits of being a dragon shifter was accelerated healing, it didn't mean that it wasn't painful as all hell. He knew the aspirin would help to take the edge off the pain shooting up his body, he had just been too damn proud before to admit that he desperately needed it.

Chase didn't know what it was exactly that had changed between them, but it seemed as if their soft banter and stolen smiles had broken the ice and eased the tension between them by tenfold, and he found himself liking their new rapport.

She watched him quietly, and he knew something was eating at her. He could practically *see* the questions rolling around in her head. He shifted to make himself a bit more comfortable as he waited for the aspirin to take effect.

"Go ahead," he urged.

"What?"

"You have questions for me," he continued, studying her face and loving the way her cheeks reddened just a bit, almost as if she had been caught with her hand in the cookie jar. "Ask whatever you'd like. I'm an open book."

MARISSA BIT BACK the squeal of delight that sprang to her lips at his generous invitation. *An open book!* She sure hoped he wasn't just yanking her tail. She had a thousand and one questions she wanted to ask of the dragon, and suddenly *Mr. Moody* was offering her free access!

It was like finding a treasure chest! One that she had better take full advantage of before he flipped once again and became the brooding jerk that she had already had the pleasure of dealing with. If there was one thing for certain, it was that Marissa wasn't going to let this chance slip through her fingers.

"You mentioned your necklace," she began.

"Amulet," he corrected her, but she didn't detect a hint of malice in his tone, he was simply correcting a fact, and she nodded quickly.

She was trying her best not to let on how excited she was, but it was hard. She was positively *bursting!* She had wanted to know about dragon shifters for as long as she could remember but had never been fortunate enough to have had the opportunity to actually *meet* one in the flesh before. It wasn't like they traveled in the same paranormal circles, and until he fully healed, this was her golden opportunity to find out as much as she could. Every and any tid-bit of information that he was willing to share.

"About your *Amulet,*" she went on, her excitement growing with each second that passed.

"Yes, what about it?"

She couldn't help but think how smooth and comforting his voice was. It was deep and even, and it made you feel instantly at ease. Well, at least it did when he wasn't being a boorish ass and snapping at her like she was an idiot out to kill him.

"I noticed that it seems to be extremely important to you, and I couldn't help but wonder why. It was the very first thing you mentioned when you woke. Well...it was once you stopped barking at me, and demanding to know who I was. Not to mention that whole *bottom feeder* remark," She finished with a smirk, and nibbled at her bottom lip to keep her grin hidden. "Is it very valuable?"

He was silent for a long moment, his brows furrowing in what seemed to be concentration, and she began to wonder if he was going to answer her or simply ignore her. Finally, after what seemed to her an eternity, he cleared his throat, and his eyes locked with hers. "It is, but only in the sense that it has been handed down for generations by my people to the leaders of the dragon clans."

Marissa felt her heart skip a beat.

Oh, Sweet Neptune's knickers! He wasn't just a dragon shifter; he was the freaking leader of the dragon shifters!

His laughter filled the air and echoed off the walls of the cavern, bouncing across the space and directly into her brain.

"I'm guessing by your somewhat stunned expression, that it would be safe to say you didn't realize that I lead my clan," he chuckled.

"I...um...no...," she stammered honestly, wondering what kind of nightmare would rain down on her and *her* people when the dragons found out that he was attacked by that group of dumbasses, and that they had tried to kill their *leader!*

It certainly would not look good for the merpeople as a whole. And from what had gathered so far, his opinion of her kind wasn't bright and shiny to begin with. This would just make it worse.

Guh!

Hadn't she heard one of them say that the amulet would be all the proof they needed to show that they had him?

What idiots! They were looking to start a war!

Deciding that it would be in her best interest not to mention his attackers and to help him, she took a deep breath and returned his gaze, squaring her shoulders with conviction.

"I had no idea, but I want you to know, that once your leg heals, and you are feeling strong enough, I'll help you find the men who did this to you. I don't want to you think that because of a few bad ones, that all my people are dishonorable thieves."

"Thank you, Marissa," he replied, and her heart once again bounced against her ribs. He hadn't called her by her name before, and the sound of it rolling past his lips caused a tingle to run across her spine, and she found herself wanting to hear him say it again. "Now, what else would you like to ask me?"

She let out a relived sigh and smiled. Her excitement growing once again by leaps and bounds.

For how long she couldn't say, but it seemed like hours, she grilled him relentlessly about dragon shifters, completely entranced by his stories, and the longer they talked the more she found herself beginning to like the big oaf in spite of herself. He was charming, and funny when he let his guard down, and she didn't even want to think about how positively sexy as hell he was!

When she had gotten most of the more pressing questions out of the way and answered to her satisfaction, he surprised her by turning the tables on her.

"Now you," he said, taking a sip from his water bottle.

"What about me?" Marissa asked innocently, honestly not having the slightest idea why he would ever want to know about her mundane little existence. He was fascinating, and she was... *nobody.*

Not to mention that the man was the leader of an ancient clan of dragons!

She wasn't stupid. She knew that most paranormal beings didn't think the merpeople were anything special. They were the keepers of the water. Left alone to watch over the oceans and black lakes. They weren't considered an important part of the supernatural realm, and it was one of the reasons her people chose to keep themselves as far from the land as possible.

There were those few over the centuries who had decided to live with the landwalkers, and those, like the men who had attacked him, who frequented the towns for their own gain and pleasure, but on land they had no powers to speak of. For all intents and purposes, they were just *human.*

Humans who happened to live forever. Human who sprouted a tail and could breathe underwater...but still human, so the other beings took great pleasure in looking down on them. Treated them no better than garbage, and she realized that was one of the main reasons why his *bottom feeders* remark had stung her so badly.

Her parents had pounded it into her head for as long as she could remember, that their place was in the sea; and those times, not so very long ago, when she *had* thrown caution to the wind and gave into her curious nature and ventured onto land had proven them right. She shoved the thought from her mind and glanced down at the cavern floor, suddenly feeling brutally exposed.

"Tell me about yourself, Marissa."

"There's nothing much to tell. I'm a mermaid. I watch over the ocean. I keep a watch over those who sail the seas. That's about it."

CHASE WATCHED THE curious little imp intently, knowing that she was holding something back. He saw a flash of something cross her features. Sadness, maybe? He couldn't be certain, but there was something below the surface with this one, and he found himself wanting to find out what it was exactly that brought that wistful look to her eyes.

He realized that he had actually enjoyed the last few hours sitting and talking with her. More than he had ever remembered enjoying anything in a very long time. Or *ever,* for that matter. This all was so not his style. He didn't sit around and *talk.* And even though, for all intents and purposes, he was on the "out of commission" list for the moment, he found himself wanting the moment to go on and on.

"You really should rest," she insisted softly, although he didn't hear much conviction in her tone at all. "I'm sure I've exhausted you with all my questions."

"I'm good, although I would kill for a cup of coffee right about now. You don't happen to have any in that magical bag of yours, do you?"

She shook her head.

"Well, then, how about another water?"

She dug around and handed him the bottle and he cracked it open.

It was better than nothing.

"You seem very," he paused, searching for the right words, "*well-schooled* in the world outside…or *above*…or however you wish to phrase it. Do you come up on land often?"

He watched her expression change instantly, as if the very thought of spending time on land brought on an overwhelming sense of…*fear*?

"Did I say something wrong?" he asked, leaning forward a bit. He winced as a shot of pain sliced through his leg and inwardly cursed his current situation.

He remained silent as she grabbed the blanket that she had used to cover herself with that morning and moved over to kneel beside him, her delicate hands easing it behind his back, and he realized that she was trying so very hard not to hurt him, and wanted to laugh.

He was a damned dragon leader, and this little set back was just a blip of nuisance in the grand scheme of things. He was getting stronger by the minute, and sure as hell didn't need a nursemaid.

Yet, as much as it irked him to admit, it was kind of nice having her tend to him.

41

He also realized something unexpected as she busied herself trying to make him comfortable.

She smelled damned amazing!

Fresh and clean, like the sea-breeze rolling off the ocean she called home, it wafted through his senses and made him forget where he was for just a millisecond in time. He caught himself leaning over to get just a bit closer to her, and breathed her scent in greedily.

She turned her head at just that moment and their mouths were suddenly mere inches apart, and it took every ounce of willpower he possessed not to follow what every single instinct he had was screaming at him, and close that tiny gap between them and steal a kiss.

Taste her lips.

Instead he cleared his throat like a complete jackass and leaned back, internally kicking himself in the ass as he did.

Just what in the hell was wrong with him? If he wanted something, he damned well took it! Deciding that he needed to rest and get the hell back to his clan, he closed his eyes and tried to ignore the sensation of the beautiful creature as she fussed over him.

CHAPTER FOUR

"I BELIEVE HE was given *the kiss* by Krill's daughter," Magnus said, watching the group's reactions closely. He had followed the maid as she had taken the dragon to her hideaway and kissed the shifter back to life. She *must* have known what a foolish risk she was taking. Not that it mattered to him in the least. All he cared about was that this information would put him in his leader's favor.

"Son of a bitch!" Aquilas shouted, throwing his mug of stout against the wall of the tavern where it exploded, sending glass shards flying in every direction. The bartender looked up with a scowl at the group of men.

The man should have figured he was due for some of this bullshit. The mermen had been much too quiet of late.

He despised the rowdy group of sea-scum. They were nothing but trouble.

But...they also paid him for the trouble they caused by ten-fold, so in the long run, the money it added to his pockets was well worth the damage that they caused. He didn't stick his nose in their business, and they stayed out of his.

"What in the *hell* was that bitch thinking?" Aquilas ranted, pacing around the deserted bar. "Does she not realize that it is not to be used on others? Damn that head-strong maid!" He seethed, walking over to stand in front of Magnus. He laid his hand on the other man's shoulder and snarled. "You've done well. Believe me when I say, it won't soon be forgotten." He turned and looked at his men, his eyes gleaming devilishly before looking back to the man standing in front of him, his chest puffed-up with pride. "Magnus, I want you to take a few of the men and keep watch on our pair," he instructed. "Make sure you do not make your presence known, just keep me abreast as to what is going on. I have some time to decide what I want to do. The shifter will need to recover from our friendly little bit of game-play. Even dragons aren't indestructible."

"Why not just do away with them both and be done with it?" Magnus asked, not much liking the fact that he was basically being assigned to play babysitter.

"Now, where would the fun in that be?" Aquilas laughed. "Who would have thought that the Princess of the Sea could be so foolish? It's a shame her father isn't still alive to see his perfect daughter's folly!"

WHEN MARISSA WAS certain that Chase had fallen asleep, she slipped through the small opening at the back of the cavern and headed toward town. They had spent the better part of the day talking and getting to know each other, and she'd found herself sharing things she hadn't shared with anyone in a very long time. If ever. She found him to be warm and caring once the *all-powerful dragon* schtick slipped away, and she found herself wanting to do something nice for him.

After much thought, she had decided that a decent supper and some coffee would be just the thing. She had checked her funds and was happy to discover that she still had more than enough to gather the supplies she needed, and set off, not numb to the fact that this would be the second time in as many days that she was going among the *landwalkers*.

Who would ever have imagined?

All it took was one ornery dragon to get her to overcome her fears. Well, if she were to be perfectly honest with herself, it wasn't *overcoming* them exactly, but at least she was forcing herself to deal with them a whole heck of a lot more than she was *before* she had rescued the man.

She strolled along; her mind lost on thoughts of the dragon leader. He had woven stories of his clan and how they worked together as brothers to serve and protect the supernatural realm, and she found herself wistfully wishing she could experience a sense a family like that.

For the most part, merpeople were notoriously self-absorbed creatures. Their beauty and grace caused them to be content in their own presence most of the time, and not really want to spend it in the company of others.

Something Marissa never could really get a grasp on.

She had always craved a connection with other creatures. She was curious by nature and had a caring heart, not to mention that she loved learning about other beings. Something her family could never truly understand.

Or condone.

Once their duty to raise their young was over, merfolk moved on.

Marissa had only heard of her father's passing by accident, and her mother had left them years before, moving on to another. As her father's only living heir, she knew she should take her place among their people to rule, she simply chose not to. Hence, her love of her secret cavern. It was her sanctuary, basically where she felt safest. And now, it was someone else's as well.

At least for the time being.

She found herself almost dreading the time when he got what he wanted from her and she led him to his attackers and then inevitably move on and went back to his people. For some reason, the idea of it caused a small pit to form in her stomach.

Marissa pushed the thought away and continued into town, unaware of the figures that lurked in the darkness watching her.

CHASE ROLLED OVER with a hearty groan of contentment and opened his eyes, pleasantly surprised that his leg didn't scream out in protest at the movement. He was getting there. Slower than he'd like, but at least he was making progress.

He sat up and glanced around for his cave-mate, surprised when he found nothing. Pushing himself up, he stood and tested his leg.

There was a dull ache, and it was still a bit weak, but things were definitely looking up.

He found himself grinning as the day spent with her flitted through his mind. Her musical laugher and quick smile. She was witty and smart, and he found himself admiring the moxie of someone who spent their time in the depths of the sea.

Now, if he could just figure out where the beautiful little sprite had run off to. Or *swam* off to, as the case may be.

He moved around a bit, stretching his legs and trying to strengthen them, before removing her make-shift splint and deciding to explore a bit.

She had to be around here somewhere.

MARISSA SLIPPED THROUGH the opening with her bag, her grin nearly cracking her face in half. She had found two wonderful looking steaks, and a camping coffee pot, and was practically bursting. It was rare that she ever ate the landwalkers fare, especially meat, so this was going to be a special treat!

"I was beginning to wonder if you had finally decided to take off and leave me to my own accord."

Marissa spun around with an audible squeak as his smooth, velvety voice drifted through the darkness. Her bag fell from her hand with a loud crash as the steel percolator slipped out of the plastic and clattered along the passageway.

"Poseidon's pufferfish!" She shrieked, glaring into the darkness. "You nearly scared the pearls right out of me! What are you doing lurking about in the dark?"

CHASE TRIED HIS damndest to hold back the ripple of laughter that was bubbling up in his gut and threatening to slip past his lips. The last thing he wanted was for her to think that he was laughing at her; but she sure as shit had a colorful way with words.

"Sorry," he choked out, trying to hide his grin as he stepped closer to where she stood, although he doubted very much that she could actually see it. He just wasn't going to take any chances. "I woke to find you gone, and decided to do a little exploring. I needed to move around a bit."

"Your leg!" She gasped, and once again he fought off the urge to laugh. He knew it had just hit her that he was standing here talking to her, instead of being laid out flat on his ass.

He sensed, more than saw, her drop down to the ground and begin to hastily gather up her supplies. He could barely make out her outline in the sparse light filtering through the cavern from the fire he had stoked back to life when he discovered her gone, but not much else at all.

"Not to worry, my leg's fine. It's healing," he told her as he moved even closer and squatted down beside her, attempting to help, but he only succeeded in knocking his chin against the top of her head with a sound snap as she scuttled about. "Shit! Sorry." He apologized, reaching out and taking her arm. "Are you alright?"

"My heads harder than you'd think," she replied, beginning to stand, and her delicate hand skimmed across his middle and rested on his hip in what must have been an attempt to steady herself. He found the contact absolutely distracting in the most delicious way and sucked in a breath.

Without conscious thought, his arm slithered around her waist and he pulled her to him, his mouth lowering and instinctively finding hers in the darkness.

He didn't give it any forethought whatsoever, or worry for a single moment about what he was doing; he was acting purely on desire and he wasn't about to listen to what common sense was trying to tell him.

As he had wandered about the cavern, searching for some sign of her, and ultimately finding nothing more than a few items stashed away, he began to feel what he could only describe as an extreme sense of loss hit him at the thought that she had finally had enough of his gruff disposition and had just simply stolen away. And, as much as it pained him to admit it, even to himself, he realized that it felt quite a bit like a punch to the gut. Something he had never experienced before in his very long life.

It had been something almost like...*panic.*

Now, his mouth greedily took hers; his tongue skimming along her lips, urging them to open, and his heart slammed against his ribs when she obliged. His free hand lifted to her face, his fingertips brushing along her cheek and caressing her warm flesh, soft as the finest of silks. A groan vibrated through his body, insisting he needed more.

Their tongues sparred and chased the others with a growing need that was impossible to deny. It was a palpable thing. Raw and demanding, and before he was fully aware of what he was doing, he had lifted her up in his arms and was walking towards the area near the fire, his mouth refusing to leave hers for even a single moment.

As if some divine presence was guiding him, he stopped where the discarded blankets lay crumpled on the floor of the cavern and gently laid her down on them, his body trembling with need as he stretched out beside her.

He knew that he should slow it down. That this was beyond crazy. But it seemed as if he had wanted this woman forever, and the taste of her mouth was the sweetest nectar that he was unable to resist.

Finally, summoning up every ounce of self-control he contained, and praying to the Gods in the Heavens to give him strength, he broke free from her mouth and looked into her eyes, those aqua depths shining like sea glass as the burning fire reflected in them, snapping and dancing as nothing he had ever seen before.

"Marissa…" he husked, not sure what it was that he wanted to say. He just knew that he needed to give her the chance to tell him to stop. To tell him that she didn't want him as much as he wanted her.

And the thought of her turning him away nearly killed him.

MARISSA GAZED UP at this man in something very much like awe, her breath hitching in her throat as his eyes seemed to stare directly into her soul, and all she wanted to do was scream…

…More.

She couldn't even begin to find the right words to express to him what she was feeling exactly. It was as if a million butterflies had been released in her tummy and her body was crying out for him in a way that was new to her.

She was so unschooled and naïve to the surge of emotions rushing through her like a whirlpool. She only knew that she didn't want it to stop. She didn't want this sublime euphoria to end, and consequences be damned!

"Chase," she husked, and the thought popped into her head that this was the first time she had called him by his name, and her mouth lifted at the corners a bit as she realized that she liked it. It sounded right. She took a quick breath as she tried to calm her pounding heart, not truly believing that this was actually happening. "Don't talk," she demanded finally. "Just shut up and kiss me."

She felt his chest vibrate against hers as he moved in closer, a cross between a laugh and a growl rumbling through him. It seemed to come from the very recesses of his soul, and his mouth slammed against hers.

Marissa's fingers skimmed up his back and into his thick, wavy hair, pulling him closer as he kissed her stupid.

She felt him tense and he broke their kiss once again, much to her distain.

"What's wrong?" she croaked as he pulled away from her, and stood.

She watched in confusion as he spun around, looking off into the darkness, his head tilted slightly as if listening for something, and she could feel the tension rolling off of him in waves. She moved and joined him, standing beside him and listening as intently.

Silence.

"Chase? What is it? What's wrong," she whispered, a growing sense of unease beginning to wash over her.

Finally, after several nerve-wracking moments of silence, he shook his head, gracing her with a small grin, and she knew that he was trying to reassure her. It seemed forced. "I thought I heard something," he replied softly. "It's nothing, I'm sure."

Marissa wondered if he had used this as an excuse to stop where their kiss was obviously leading, and swallowed back her mortification.

She cleared her throat and began to gather her forgotten bags, trying to find something to busy herself with in the hopes of hiding her embarrassment.

"Oh! I almost forgot," she rushed out, and found herself beginning to ramble on like a fool before she could stop herself. "I…um, I got stuff for dinner and…and I got coffee."

His chuckle drifted through the air and warmed her belly as he helped her to gather their supplies and head back to the fire. He moved around searching for driftwood as she began to prepare what she hoped would be an edible meal, wondering if his sudden change of heart was because he had come to his senses and knew that getting involved with her was a mistake, and completely beneath him.

He was a dragon leader. A warrior. He had no business consorting with the likes of her.

CHASE WATCHED HER as he moved about, his curiosity piqued as to why she was suddenly so flustered.

After much deliberation, he realized that she must have been confused by his abrupt ending to their kiss when she had obviously not heard what he had, and he found that he wanted to reassure her that it had not been by choice, but he just couldn't bring himself to do it.

He had no right to kiss her as he had. It damn well wasn't the right time, nor place. His basic desire had gotten the better of him and had distracted him, causing him to let his defenses down, *again*. Something he should have learned the hard way that he should never do. Especially considering his current situation. He wasn't about to go down that road again.

He *knew* that he had heard *something*. It had been faint, almost like the sound of a soft cough. He was fairly certain of it;

yet couldn't help but wonder if it had merely been his subconscious telling him he needed to stop.

No matter how much he hadn't wanted to.

His priority needed to be concentrating on finding the men who had done this to him. He wanted to get his Amulet of Dragaan back, and return to his clan. They would begin to wonder where he had gone, and a beautiful mermaid was just the distraction he sure as hell didn't need at the moment. He had been searching for, what he now believed to be, this very group of men who were attacking paranormals; robbing and killing them at will, and he was not about to stop now that he was so close to ending them.

He glanced over at the lovely creature in question as she busied herself preparing their meal and felt a strange ache begin in his chest.

She was exquisite.

He thanked the Gods that she had found it within herself to lend him assistance. Not to mention that if he were to be completely honest, she was just the lead he had needed to find these bastards and end their reign of terror once and for all.

It was almost as if fate had stepped in.

A small part of him felt guilty for using her this way, but the one thing Chase had learned over his many years of leading was that you never looked a gift horse...or *fish*...in the mouth.

He sure as shit didn't need to muddy the waters by toying with her emotions simply because she was just too hard to resist for her own good...or his! It wasn't her fault that she was perfection personified.

He grabbed what driftwood he could find and brought it over to the fire. He sat down beside her and gave her a wayward smile.

"It smells delicious," he commented, suddenly at a loss for what to say to her.

Christ! She was distracting as hell.

All he could focus on was the overwhelming desire to pull her back into his arms and kiss her until they were both out of breath and senseless. His body cried out for it.

He really needed to focus.

"YOU STUPID, IGNORANT son of a bitch!" Magnus growled in fury, grabbing Dimitri by the neck and throwing him against a nearby tree with a powerful crack. "You could have just screwed everything up!"

"I wasn't thinking," he pushed out as he gasped for much needed air.

Magnus had him in a death grip, fighting with every ounce of restraint he had not to just snap the bastard's neck, knowing that Dimitri's ignorance could have cost them dearly.

The boy *hadn't* been thinking. He'd been day-dreaming. Wishing he were in some woman's bed instead of keeping watch on a dragon leader and freaking *Ariel!*

"No. You were not." Magnus countered angrily, easing his hold on him a bit. "Luckily, we seem to be in the clear. I suggest we go report back to Aquilas and see what he wants us to do next." He glanced toward the small opening that Krill's daughter had slipped through. "I doubt they will be leaving anytime soon."

He dropped his hand and Dimitri slid down to his knees in the dirt, greedily pulling air into his lungs. He'd had his fill of this group of mermen. At first, he had found enjoyment in robbing and ridding their world of other beings. It made him feel superior. Not to mention lined his pockets and granted him the ability to buy and live a way that a mer never could have imagined.

But now…it was beginning to get out of hand. They were *actually* beginning to believe all this hype they were selling.

Yes. It had been thrilling and prosperous, but it was just getting old now. They were getting careless, and the fact that they had tried to kill a leader of a powerful dragon clan was just foolhardy and arrogant.

Dimitri had done some homework, and the dragon in question was a powerful and important man. Not to mention the rumors that he was also looking for *them*.

Shit and hellfire! What in the name of Poseidon had Aquilas been thinking? Although, he doubted very much that Aquilas had truly known what and *who* they had been messing with.

Now, thanks to the daughter of Krill, the dragon was still alive! Where in the *hell* had she come from?

He looked up at Magnus who was staring down at him in what could only be described as pure contempt, and decided that he was done. No more. He would leave this group of pirates at the first opportunity. He was done killing and stealing from others. He was done listening to the bullshit these men spewed about being the superior species.

He was just done.

"Get up," Magnus sneered in disgust before turning and walking away.

CHAPTER FIVE

"I HAVE TO give you credit, Sweetheart," Chase sighed, feeling more content then he had in years. He leaned back and took a long swig of his coffee. "You did one hell of a fine job on dinner considering that you live underwater most of the time."

He watched her eyes light up at his compliment and it hit him how absolutely striking she was. Her flawless alabaster skin and heart-shaped face were things most men could only dream about. Her lips were plump and pink, and they glistened in the firelight as if begging to be tasted again.

And, by God, he wanted more than anything to just throw caution to the wind and give in to the gnawing need that was pulling at his gut.

Instead he cleared his throat and took another sip of his coffee.

"So, tell me," he said, trying hard to distract himself by any means possible. "What exactly about living on land doesn't appeal to you?" He didn't know why he cared to know; he just knew that he did.

She was silent for a very long time, almost as if debating on whether to answer him or not, and he found himself not liking the look that suddenly appeared behind her eyes. It was much like that of a caged or cornered animal.

His curiosity piqued, he leaned forward a bit and captured her gaze, trying his best to give her a reassuring smile. He didn't understand why he was so...*protective* of her. He was a leader. He usually didn't go the gentle route.

But with her...

"Marissa, you can tell me," he urged.

MARISSA TRIED TO force back the lump forming in her throat as the sound of her name leaving his lips wrapped around her. Good Lord, but the man's voice was like a soothing balm that just instantly eased her soul. It slithered across her body and made her want to do whatever he asked of her, and before she could even think to stop herself, the words were spilling from her mouth in a heated rush.

"I've never really felt like I belonged anywhere," she said, her voice low. "My father was a leader who never had time for me, and my mother left not long after I was born. Merpeople are nomadic by nature, and family isn't very important to most. I never felt that way. I found myself longing for a family, and as I grew, I thought that maybe I would fit in better on land. Perhaps find what I was missing. I had heard so many stories of others who had chosen that life." She hesitated a moment, feeling as if she needed to explain that not all her people were scum. "Merpeople, like the men who attacked you, but...also others. Good people, who simply wanted a life away from the waters." She took a shaky breath, looking down at her hands as she twisted them in her lap. "I never really planned to stay above the water. I thought I would simply venture on land from time to time, experiencing whatever I could. There were so many amazing things to do and see, and I was fascinated by it. That was when I began to stash away money and clothes and the necessities that I knew would be needed to fit in. This way, I could move among the landwalkers undetected and learn all about their way of life."

Marissa stopped, feeling as if a very large stone had been placed on her chest. It felt as if the air had thickened around her, and she tried to take a calming breath. She hadn't realized that this would be so difficult.

"I was walking alone late one night, and I passed a pub. I guess I must have been unconsciously drawn to the sounds of laughter coming from inside. It was intoxicating. I stopped to watch a moment, listening to the music as it filled the air. As I stood there, almost transfixed by the sight of people dancing, there was a trio of men who were being thrown out for what I can only assume was drunkenness. I realized that it would be in my best interest to keep walking and I quickly continued on, not wanting be noticed.

But it was too late, and they began to follow me."

She stopped, feeling as if her throat was closing up on her and realized that it was because of the tears that were stinging the backs of her eyes. Threatening to spill out, and she tried to will them away. That night had been horrendous. They had taunted and grabbed at her, and she had come as close to being violated as she had ever been. She hadn't had anyone to run to for help. Luckily, the sound of someone coming had caught their attention enough that she had been able to break away and run.

And run she had. Like the Devil himself were chasing her.

Marissa *knew* how lucky she had been that night, and had all but stopped venturing on land after that unless it was absolutely necessary, realizing that the creatures who lived there were dangerous and vile.

"Let's just say that I was fortunate enough to have been able to refuse their advances and leave them behind in one piece, but they really didn't leave a great impression of landwalkers on me," she choked out, shaking her head and looking back up to meet his gaze. The compassion that she saw reflected in his eyes nearly stole the breath from her lungs. It was honest and genuine.

She caught her breath and watched in stunned silence as he leaned forward and grasped her arm, pulling her toward him so that she was suddenly nestled firmly on his lap as he wrapped his strong arms around her. His biceps felt like steel bands around her as he held her to his chest, and she felt safer than she could ever remember feeling before.

"Chase…" his name was no more than a whisper coming from her lips, but he didn't say a word. He simply tilted his head and leaned forward, silencing whatever she had been planning to say with his mouth on hers.

Not that she had even the slightest inkling as to what she *was* going to say, but it didn't matter. The moment his lips met hers, all rational thought flew out of her head and she kicked into running on pure instinct and desire.

She kissed him back greedily, *hungrily*, without a moment's hesitation, making sure to convey to him that she wanted this as much as he seemed to.

Their tongues tasted and teased the others in a sensual game of tag that had an urgency and demand that had her skin humming with excitement. Marissa's blood rushed through her veins and her body ached for so much more, even though she wasn't quite sure what that actually was.

She only knew that she never wanted this feeling to end.
Ever.

Her throat vibrated with an unspoken protest when he leaned back and broke away from her greedy mouth, his eyes capturing hers and holding. She swore that she heard him audibly swallow.

Marissa stared back at him in silence as she once again realized how devastatingly handsome he was. Strong and powerful, his perfect jawline was defined and squared with just a hint of scruff, which only served to enhance the dangerousness of his looks to toe-curling perfection. Thick, dark hair and eyes the color of quicksilver. He made her want things she hadn't even realized she wanted before, and although the very thought should have frightened her senseless…it didn't. It only caused her pulse to race and her confidence to soar. She knew beyond a doubt that she was in good hands.

It was as if she had been created solely for this purpose. And as crazy as it sounded in her head, she knew in her heart that it was true. This was meant to happen. She was meant to find him that night.

Destined.

"Marissa, I want you to…"

She stopped him with a finger pressed to his lips and a small shake of her head. She didn't want to talk. She didn't want to analyze and think about where this might or might not lead. She wanted only to, for once in her long, miserable life, let herself go and just enjoy the moment.

She reclaimed his mouth, pressing herself blatantly against him as if her very existence depended on it, and she felt, more than heard, him groan, his chest vibrating against hers and causing her body to shiver as a tingle of pure desire slid up her body, coiling itself around her and filling her was liquid heat.

Before she could even begin to comprehend what was happening, he twisted his massive body so that she was lying on her back on the blankets that lay in a crumpled mound on the floor, his own muscular form pressing up against hers as his hands began roaming her body as she had so wished they'd do.

And it was everything she had imagined...*and more.*

His skilled, strong fingers slid across her skin and down her leg, whispering against her flesh and leaving a trail of white-hot heat wherever they happened to venture.

And venture they did.

He gripped the hem of her sundress and slid it up...up until there was no other choice but to release his mouth so that he could slip it from her body before tossing it across the cave with a soft *whoosh* of fabric.

She experienced a split second where she wondered if she should feel embarrassed or shy, but it quickly passed. The only thought running through her mind was: *why am I naked and you're not!*

Planning to rectify the situation posthaste, her fingers traveled across his incredible chest and down over his tight stomach to his waist. She deftly pulled his shirt up and over his head without a moment's hesitation and tossed it to where she was sure her sundress lay. She felt him shiver when her hand made its way back down to the button of his jeans.

He groaned deep in his gut as she boldly unfastened the button, taking in a quick breath as her hand brushed against his erection which was fighting valiantly against the constraints of the fabric.

With a growl that sent a ripple of desire rushing across her, he moved and slipped out of them in record time, moving back and pulling her into his arms once more.

Heaven.

CHASE WAS FAIRLY sure that he was going explode right then and there as the little imp's hands moved across his body. The sensation one of pure sensory overload.

The Gods knew that he had been with his fair share of women over the years, but this beautiful vixen was…*different.* Different in a way that was throwing him for a loop. She fired his blood as no one else ever had, and his mind was going in a million different directions all at once.

A part of him was screaming at him to slow down. That she had been through a lot, and he needed to go easy with her. Not to mention that he really didn't need this type of entanglement in his life. He was a loner. A leader who didn't share himself with anyone. But his body was aching to touch, feel, *experience* every freaking single inch of her silken flesh.

It was one of the hardest battles he had ever fought, and when in that next instant, her warm lips made contact with his shoulder and placed tiny kisses there and up his neck as her fingers scraped across his stomach, he knew he was lost. There was no fighting, nor denying the need coursing through him any longer. He just swore to himself to take is easy with her.

That was, if he could.

He returned the favor and nibbled at the pulse beating wildly in her throat, loving the feeling of it as it fluttered against his lips, not to mention the sweet taste of her skin. It was sublime. He made his way down, taking great pains not to miss a single inch of flesh as he kissed his way across her collarbone and down to the valley between her breasts, reveling in the soft mewling sounds coming from her as he did.

Chase knew, in the pit of his stomach, that this woman was pure, and that she needed to be cherished. He reminded himself once again, to go slow. He didn't want to frighten her.

His mouth made contact with her breast, moving from one taut peak to the other, before tracing his tongue down her stomach and around her belly button before playfully dipping inside and pulling a sexy as hell gasp from her that did nothing to ease his raging libido.

He glanced up and met her passion drugged gaze as she gave him a knowing smile. With a groan of pure desire, he moved between her thighs, his mouth taking possession of her honeyed sweetness. His tongue tasted and teased, causing a cry of desperation to escape her, and he was vaguely aware of her fingers slipping into his hair and pulling him closer as his teeth nipped and toyed the tiny bud of her womanhood. It was only a moment later that he felt her hit her peak, and she cried out. His name flying past her lips in a husky rush as he continued to work his magic until her body stopped convulsing and relaxed. Although he could still feel her tiny quakes of contentment.

"Chase," she almost begged, and it was sexy as hell, "*more.*"

He moved his body so that he was above her, his arms straining to keep his full weight off of her as the rock-hard proof of his desire made its presence known between them.

"Marissa," breathed, his voice no more than a hoarse whisper. "I don't want to frighten you."

She stared into his eyes for what seemed an eternity before her face lit up with a smile that could have outshone the brightest of stars in the night sky. It was beautiful. It was powerful.

It was *magical.*

And if very nearly did him in.

"You don't frighten me, Chase," she said with a confidence that was awe-inspiring.

"I'll hurt you when I come into you," he responded, trying his best to be considerate, something he had never worried about before tonight.

She nibbled at her bottom lip a moment, her eyes sparkling with what seemed to be a bit of mischief mixed with undeniable passion. "You'll hurt me if you don't," she replied finally, and he felt his heart seize up in his chest.

The little minx was going to kill him.

With every single ounce of restraint that he possessed, he moved so that he could join their bodies, taking the utmost care to go as slowly as was possible and give her time to adjust to him. He felt her barrier and stilled, hating that he would need to cause her even the slightest amount of pain, but this astounding woman merely wrapped her legs around him and with a small wince, he was buried in her to the hilt.

He stilled, attempting to give her a moment, but by the Gods – she wasn't having it. With another saucy little grin that did something undefinable to his heart, she began to move beneath him, and his breath was quite literally ripped right from his lungs.

Chase slammed his eyes shut as he began to move his body, matching the rhythm of hers to perfection, slowly at first, but with increasing intensity as she urged him on, his name slipping from her lips over and over again on a sigh.

Just when he thought he could hold back not a second longer, he felt her orgasm slam through her once again and her body tightened around him.

He let himself go, reaching that euphoric release right along with her.

It was like nothing he could have ever imagined or hoped to experience in his lifetime. These feelings just didn't happen to him.

And…it scared the ever-loving piss out of him. This woman was different. She was…*everything*.

MARISSA BIT DOWN on her lip so hard that she tasted blood as she tried to quell the scream that was threatening to burst from her as her body was wracked with the most astounding sensation. It was like being caught in the heart of a tidal wave and being tossed and turned in every direction all at once.

It was staggering.

He moved to lay beside her and pulled her into the crook of his arm and tightly into his embrace, as if afraid she might take off, which was the furthest thing on her mind at the moment.

She happily snuggled against his chest; her ear pressed to where his heart was pounding rhythmically against his ribs. She smiled as she listened to it begin to ease itself into the steady tempo that was so darn comforting.

"So, tell me more about your people," she whispered with contentment. Wanting to know as much about him as he was willing to offer. "Who gave you your amulet?" She asked.

She was aware of his lips kissing the top of her head as he wriggled to make himself more comfortable before reaching over to grab the extra blanket to throw over their cooling bodies.

She fought back a giggle, not wanting him to think she was nuts, but she was positively giddy!

"It was my father's," he replied on a yawn, and she realized that he had to be exhausted. He still wasn't fully healed and had just used up quite a bit of energy. "He presented it to me as his father before him had done to him, and so on," he continued, and she could hear the weariness in his words as he spoke. "It's not that it holds any special powers or is innately valuable, it is just given to each leader when he takes over the clan. It's an age-old tradition that has been upheld for centuries. I wished to one day give it to my son."

She felt her stomach flip at that one. Did he have a wife? Children? Oh, God! What had she done?

Almost as if reading her thoughts, he squeezed her a little tighter to him. "*When* I have a son of my own."

Feeling about a thousand percent better with his words, she let herself relax. "Traditions are important," she noted softly. "My father led our people for many years. Well, for what that is really worth. For the most part, merpeople are solitary creatures by nature, so there really wasn't much to rule."

"I've heard as much." He agreed. "But you don't seem to fit into that mold," he observed with another soft kiss to her temple this time.

"I am…for the most part. I'm just particular on whose company I keep."

"Mm," he chuckled, his voice thick with drowsiness. "I hope I made the grade."

"You have."

"Good."

She could feel his breathing beginning to even out as he drifted off to sleep and couldn't help but smile when her cheek began to vibrate as he started to snore.

Marissa lay there for a very long while, content as a clam, reliving the moment in her mind over and over. As much as she hated to admit it, she realized that she liked the man.

Really liked him. More than she probably should.

She had no idea what tomorrow would bring, but she wasn't about to worry about it. She couldn't. It would drive her insane. She was just going to enjoy the moment, and let things happen as they may.

Deciding that sleep was not going to come anytime soon, she slipped from his arms and quietly crept over to where he had tossed her sundress, deciding that she would sneak back into town and pick up something for the morning.

Something special.

Hopefully the young girl at the store would be working and would help her decide what to get. She'd seemed nice enough the last few times Marissa had ventured there.

Maybe she could even find something else to wear. Something nice. She bit back the squeal of excitement and silently headed for the opening, grabbing her last bit of money as she did and trying to keep herself from dancing all the way.

CHAPTER SIX

MARISSA LEFT THE shop with a newfound spring to her step as she held her purchases tightly against her chest. She was positively walking on air as she made her way back toward her little hideaway.

Their hideaway, she silently corrected herself, and allowed herself a moment or two of unguarded fancy to just enjoy the feeling of jubilation that the thought evoked. It was like a slap of happiness straight to the face, and she found that she wanted it to go on forever.

No matter what her common sense was whispering to her.

She wasn't dumb. She *knew* that this couldn't last, and she wasn't about to lie to herself and pretend that it could.

No matter how much she may have wanted it to.

She found that the admission really didn't take her by surprise. She knew she was beginning to have feelings for the strong-willed dragon.

Strong feelings.

Feelings that were frightening, yet exhilarating all at the same time and were making her head spin. But, if nothing else, Marissa was also a realist, and knew that she didn't fit into his world.

He was a leader of dragons. Strong. Powerful. Important.

A man who, she was sure, needed to get back to his people. She was nothing more to him than a distraction to entertain him while he healed. Well, *that* and to be his one and only hope at the moment of finding the men he was looking for.

As she neared the entrance to the cave, she had the sudden and overwhelming feeling of being watched. That subtle, but uneasy sense of something creeping along your spine and making the hairs at the back of your neck tingle. She quickened her pace a bit, wanting nothing more than to crawl back into the safety of Chase's arms and perhaps get some sleep.

She chanced a quick glance back and swore she saw a shadow dart behind tree, then another, but couldn't be sure. It could have simply been a play of the moonlight filtering through the clouds. She took a breath, eyeing the crevice to the cavern on a few yards away, and tried not to panic.

She must just be overtired. The past few days had been exhausting is so many ways. Both good and bad.

She was no more than twenty feet from the small opening when a voice from coming from behind stopped her cold.

"Daughter of Krill, this is truly an unexpected surprise. Who would have ever thought you would be foolish enough to interfere in our affairs? Such beauty. It's a shame you have nothing going on upstairs."

Marissa spun around to find three men standing behind her, partially hidden within the darkness of the shadows, but she knew immediately who they were, and she felt her blood turn to ice. She took a small step back, preparing to run when an arm wrapped around her waist and the other across her chest in a death grip.

The cry of terror that started to fly past her lips was abruptly cut off by the intensity of his hold, knocking the air straight out of her with a mighty *whoosh*.

"Not so rough, Magnum," the leader instructed, although she could hear the humor in his voice. These men knew nothing other than rough, and the bastard holding onto her only tightened his grip. "It has come to my attention that you took it upon yourself to save the dragon shifter we had, shall we say, *disposed* of. And that you were actually stupid enough to bestow upon him, *The Kiss*."

Marissa glared back at him, her body trembling with fury. "You are nothing but disgusting filth!" She hissed, struggling to free herself and wanting nothing more than to lunge at him and gouge his eyes out. "You and your cronies are boils on the asses of decent people!"

The group of men laughed.

"That may be," he replied with a snort, "but, we choose our paths as we see fit. Much as you have chosen yours. And now you must pay the price, I'm afraid."

Marissa growled in pure hatred as she did her best to lash out, and was somewhat pleased when she managed to deliver a quick kick to her captures shin. It didn't give her any leeway towards escape, but his soft grunt of pain *did* give her a glimmer of satisfaction.

"She is a feisty little thing," the man holding her laughed. "I say we keep her around for a bit, Aquilas. I'm sure we could have some fun with her."

"Outstanding idea," he agreed. "Once we dispose of the dragon once and for all, we'll celebrate." He walked up to stand in front of her and ran his finger along her cheek, causing her to flinch just as a mighty roar filled the air.

Everyone turned, their expressions filled with shock as the silvery dragon moved closer, and Marissa knew in an instant that it was Chase. She would know those eyes anywhere.

She took the opportunity at hand, and pulled free from Magnus's hold and slamming into Aquilas, knocking him off balance as she moved away from the group of stunned mermen.

She looked to Chase, in awe of the beautiful creature standing so magnificently before them, his iridescent scales sparkling as if they were made of diamonds in the light of the moon, and understood instantly what he meant when he tossed his mighty head in the direction of the cavern.

She gave him a knowing smile and took off running.

The night sky lit up with an orange glow as a burst of flame exploded just as she was about to step through the crevice sand she paused, turning to and stare at it a moment in wonder before slipping through and waiting, pacing back and forth near the opening.

What seemed to be an eternity passed and Marissa was just about to lose her battle with patience and run back outside when Chase finally made his way through the opening in all his splendid glory. Huge, powerful...her heart jumped to her throat and she couldn't have stopped herself from launching her body into his arms if she had tried.

"Now, that's what I call a proper greeting," he laughed, wrapping his arms around her in return. He tilted his head and took her mouth to which she responded to him ten-fold.

When they finally pulled back, both were breathing hard and she felt dizzy. The passion that seemed to flare up between them had her head spinning, and she loved it!

"You were unbelievable," she mused, smiling so hard that her cheeks were beginning to ache.

"It was nothing," he laughed.

"Are they...gone?"

He nodded before leaning down and taking her lips again. "Whatever possessed you to sneak out?" He whispered against her mouth, although his tone was not in the least bit accusatory.

Marissa felt her cheeks heat. "I wanted to get something special for the morning, and a change of clothes." She realized that her purchases lay somewhere out there and were most likely nothing more than ashes. She sighed. "Speaking of clothes," she went on, smiling coyly. "You aren't wearing any."

"Yes, and you are," he countered with a devilish grin. "I do believe we should remedy that immediately. Even out the playing field, so to say."

In the next instant, he had her dress pulled up over her head and had swept her up in his arms, striding confidently toward their makeshift bed.

"I promise you, once we get back to my clan, you'll have a real bed," he husked, laying her down and beginning to place tiny kisses along her skin, causing a delightful ripple of electricity to run across her body.

"Are you asking me to come live with you?" She rasped in wonder, trying her best to concentrate on what he was saying and *not* the exquisite sensation of his warm mouth on her skin as he continued to tease her.

He stopped what he was doing and looked up at her, capturing her gaze in the embers of their blazing fire. "I am. No more of this solitary life, *mermaid*. You'll have a family. My clan is loud and rough, but they are also faithful, and will welcome you with open arms."

Marissa watched him in silence, her heart pounding so hard that she feared it would explode.

"Marissa," he went on softly. "I'm asking you to come home with me. To build a life with me. I know it seems impossible, but I am steadfastly falling in love with you, and can't imagine going on another day without you by my side." He placed a kiss against her lips, and she felt the world spinning and twirling around her. "Do you think you can handle living a life on land with a band of rowdy dragons and their leader who promises to cherish and love you for eternity?"

Marissa's eyes welled with tears and she nodded her head, the gesture shaking them free to roll down her cheeks. "Yes, I can," she croaked, and Chase let out a whoop that made her giggle with absolute happiness. She hugged him to her, burying her face in his neck and inhaling his scent greedily.

How she could have fallen so thoroughly, and so quickly for this man was a mystery, but she had.

And she knew beyond a shadow of a doubt that should would love him in return.

Forever.

"Oh!" She squeaked, leaning back. "Your amulet! It must have been lost when you...took care of those scum. One of them must have had it."

Chase laughed, before nuzzling her neck in the most distracting way, and she moaned.

"It doesn't matter," he whispered against her skin and she felt gooseflesh break out. "I have something *much* better."

And with that, he proved to her just how much he meant it.

ABOUT THE AUTHOR

DARLENE KUNCYTES WAS born and raised in Northeast Ohio and still happily resides there with her spoiled rotten fur-babies. She has loved losing herself to reading and writing for as long as she can remember and has always had a special place in her heart for romance. She's got a wicked sense of humor who loves to find the humor in everyday life and believes that anything is absolutely possible as long as you believe it is! And, yes...she is exceedingly, and sometimes disgustingly happy! Life is way too short to waste a moment of it hating!

She is currently hard at work on the fourth novel in The Supernatural Desire Series – Harper's Heavenly Embrace!

You can find all of Darlene's books on Amazon and at Barnes and Noble.

For more information on Darlene, visit her at:

WWW.DARLENEKUNCYTES.COM

Made in the USA
Columbia, SC
06 May 2024

34955518R00048